CINDERELLA
and the
INCREDIBLE TECHNO-SLIPPERS

BY CHARLOTTE AND ADAM GUILLAIN

ILLUSTRATED BY BECKA MOOR

Curious Fox

This story is based on the fairy tale Cinderella. There are several versions of the story including ones from Jacob Grimm (1785–1863) and Wilhelm Grimm (1786–1859), Charles Perrault (1628–1703), and Giambattista Basile (1566–1632).

Perhaps the most famous version is as follows. A girl's mother dies and her father remarries. His new wife has two daughters who make the girl work in the kitchen and call her Cinderella, because she is always dirty from the ashes from the fire. When her stepsisters are invited to a royal ball, Cinderella is told she can't go. However, she is helped by a fairy godmother and goes to the ball, where nobody recognizes her. She dances with the prince, but leaves a slipper behind as she runs away at the end. The prince takes the slipper to find Cinderella. In some versions of the tale, it is the birds that show him the way. The slipper fits and the two of them live happily ever after at the palace.

First published in 2015 by Curious Fox,
an imprint of Capstone Global Library Limited,
264 Banbury Road, Oxford, OX2 7DY
Registered company number: 6695582

www.curious-fox.com

Text copyright © Charlotte and Adam Guillain 2015
Illustrations by Becka Moor

ISBN 978 1 782 02314 2
19 18 17 16 15
10 9 8 7 6 5 4 3 2 1

A CIP catalogue for this book is available from the British Library.

Printed and bound in China.

CAST OF CHARACTERS

CINDERELLA

CINDERELLA'S DAD

CINDERELLA'S STEPMOTHER

TOBY AND TARA, THE STEPMOTHER'S TWINS

THE TOY FACTORY OWNER

Cinderella lived happily with her inventor Dad.

But when Dad got re-married, things turned...

Her stepmother's
twins made a mess
of everything!
They took
Cinderella's toys
and broke the lot.

But Cinderella took the broken
pieces to built cool robots and ...

... a pair of incredible techno-slippers.

So when Dad lost his job at the
toy factory, Cinderella really
wanted to cheer him up at the
closing down party.

It would be the perfect place to dance in her techno-slippers!

Unfortunately...

But cool robots can find cool things.

Soon Cinderella was whooshing off to the party on her homemade skateboard....

Nobody noticed Cinderella
arriving at the party.

She twirled and whirled on the dancefloor in her incredible techno-slippers!

Cinderella was the best dancer at the party!

The factory owner gasped, "Those slippers are amazing!" But then the clock struck midnight and...

DING DONG!

Cinderella left in such a rush, one of her slippers slipped off.

"I need to find the inventor
of this incredible slipper,"
the factory owner cheered.

"The person who made it shall have a job right here!"

Nobody could get the techno-slipper to work.

I can't turn it on!

'Why don't you try it on?'
the factory owner asked Cinderella.

It was a perfect fit!

Cinderella put on both slippers
and began to dance.

...that she saved the toy factory.

And Cinderella was now far too busy to clean up other people's mess!